Ivana the Inventor

Damon Burnard

Collins

Look out for more *Jets* from Collins

Jessy Runs Away • *Best Friends* • **Rachel Anderson**
Ivana the Inventor • *Ernest the Heroic Lion Tamer* • **Damon Burnard**
Two Hoots • *Almost Goodbye Guzzler* • **Helen Cresswell**
Shadows on the Barn • **Sarah Garland**
Nora Bone • *The Mystery of Lydia Dustbin's Diamonds* • **Brough Girling**
Thing on Two Legs • *Thing in a Box* • **Diana Hendry**
Desperate for a Dog • *More Dog Trouble* • **Rose Impey**
Georgie and the Dragon • *Georgie and the Planet Raider* • **Julia Jarman**
Cowardy Cowardy Cutlass • *Free With Every Pack* • **Robin Kingsland**
Mossop's Last Chance • *Mum's the Word* • **Michael Morpurgo**
Hiccup Harry • *Harry Moves House* • **Chris Powling**
Rattle and Hum, Robot Detectives • **Frank Rodgers**
Our Toilet's Haunted • **John Talbot**
Rhyming Russell • *Messages* • **Pat Thomson**
Monty the Dog Who Wears Glasses • *Monty's Ups and Downs* • **Colin West**
Ging Gang Goolie, it's an Alien • *Stone the Crows, it's a Vacuum Cleaner* •
Bob Wilson

First published by A & C Black Ltd in 1995
Published by Collins in 1996
10 9 8 7 6 5 4
Collins is an imprint of HarperCollins*Publishers* Ltd,
77–85 Fulham Palace Road, Hammersmith, London W6 8JB

ISBN 0 00 675201 2

Text and illustrations © Damon Burnard 1995

Damon Burnard asserts the moral right to
be identified as the author and the illustrator of the work.
A CIP record for this title is available from the British Library.
Printed and bound in Great Britain by Clays Ltd, St Ives plc

Chapter 1

At number twenty-one Dripping
Street, in the town of Hogsville,
there lives a boy who can turn
people to stone, by saying their
name backwards while standing on
his head. But this story isn't about
him. It's about the girl next door at
number twenty-three.

Her name is Ivana.

From the day she was born, Ivana was remarkable. She wasn't like other babies at all. For example, when ordinary babies are hungry, they say something like this:

But when Ivana was hungry, she'd say something like this:

While ordinary babies look at books like this . . .

. . . Ivana looked at books like these . . .

Einstein

Mumbo Jumbo

Gobbledy

GOOK

What is ARt?

The history of THINGs

cognitive development

Atoms Schmatoms

ERNest tHE HEROic Lion tAmeR

GendeR and Sexuality

PLAto

SAuceRo

Civilization; is it much good, Really?

DRIPPY Poets

REAlly complicated stuff About SCIENCE volume 1062

And while ordinary babies keep
their mums and dads awake by
crying all night, Ivana kept hers
awake by discussing astronomy . . .

At first, Ivana's mum and dad were
very distressed. They thought
having a baby would be fun, and
that it wouldn't be cleverer than
them until it was at least eight
or nine!

They tried everything to keep Ivana amused, but it was no use. She became bored with her toys after just a few minutes . . .

. . . and she wasn't good with children her own age.

Ivana's parents had completely run out of ideas when, just before her fifth birthday . . .

They laced up their boots, pulled on their coats and ran out to get one that very afternoon.

Chapter 2

Within seconds of opening her
present, Ivana began to invent.
First she invented a blue splodge
which burned a hole in the floor.

Next she invented a really
bad smell.

And then came her first great invention, which is still talked about to this day.

By heating, mixing, droozling and flixing some chemicals, Ivana made a green powder. Then she added a drop of water . . .

. . . and . . .

. . . it turned into an instant baby-sitter!

Suddenly, Ivana's parents thought that having a genius for a daughter wasn't so bad after all! From then on, they went out whenever they wanted to and for as long as they wished, without ever worrying about Ivana.

11

Instant baby-sitters were just the beginning. By the time Ivana was nine, she had invented incalculable, innovative, ingenious inventions. For example . . .

. . . heat sensitive sausages . . .

. . . crash helmets for fleas . . .

. . . an alarm clock for heavy sleepers . . .

. . . and the remote-controlled shadow.

Chapter 3

One morning, Ivana was in her laboratory putting the finishing touches to her latest invention; a mechanical dog named Chester.

To celebrate, she decided to take Chester out for a walk. As she strolled through the streets of Hogsville, she watched people reading their morning papers.

'Gosh!' she observed.

Ivana was usually too busy inventing to bother with the news. But today she picked up a copy of *The Hogsville Herald* and had a look.

'Quivering quarks!' she exclaimed.

On the gardening page it said that a shortage of rain had turned the lawns of Bedfordshire, Buckinghamshire and Berkshire brown.

'Oh dear!' Ivana sighed. And then she turned to the sports page. 'Hmm . . . I see that City beat United in the cup 10–0!'

Ivana decided to do something
about this terrible state of affairs.

Quick as a flash,
    she raced
        back home.

Chapter 4

Back in the laboratory, Ivana
gathered together all the things
she needed.

Before Ivana could start inventing,
she had to put on her Lucky
Thinking Cap.

But her laboratory was so full of
clutter, it was impossible to find
anything.

This is what Ivana's Lucky
Thinking Cap looks like.

Can you help her find it?

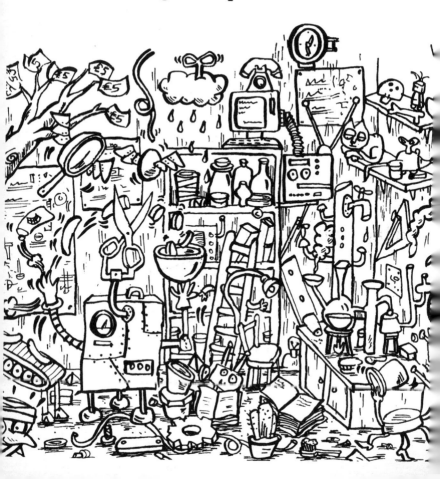

Now that she had her cap, Ivana locked the door and got down to some serious inventing.

Three days later she emerged with a big smile on her face.

Chapter 5

Ivana telephoned the News Editor of *The Hogsville Herald* and invited him round for tea. Gloomily he accepted.

'And bring the Sports Editor and the Gardening Editor with you!' said Ivana the Inventor.

Author's note: In case you don't know, an editor is someone who decides what goes into a newspaper or book, and what does not. Editors have big, black pens which they use to cross out words they don't like. Take the editor of this book, for example, who is a ~~wonderful~~ ~~wise~~ if you ask me!

When her guests had arrived, Ivana made her announcement. 'Ladies and Gentlemen!' she announced.

I've just invented some ink which will make The Hogsville Herald the world's most popular paper!

'Oh really?' said the News Editor, taking a bite from a pork pie.

'See for yourselves!' Ivana boasted.

'But there's nothing on it!' hissed the News Editor, snatching the empty sheet of paper.

'Look closer,' Ivana insisted.
And they did.

Suddenly, before their very eyes,
words appeared on the page!
'Hey! Look here!' the News Editor
spluttered.

The Sports Editor
snatched the sheet.

'You're both nuts!' the Gardening Editor scoffed.

It was all very confusing and before long, everyone was arguing at the tops of their voices about what the sheet of paper said.

yelled Ivana. 'I can explain.'

'In other words,' said Ivana,

The News Editor was so overjoyed,
he ate a huge Polish sausage.

Then he rushed home to tell his
daughter, Annie, the good news.

Page 27 may look blank, but in fact
it's been printed with Ivana's
transmogrificational ink! To make
it work, stare at the page, think of
something nice and concentrate
really, really hard. Good luck!

Chapter 6

boomed the News Editor, as he
crashed through the door.

said Annie, suspiciously.

'Ivana the Inventor has made some ink which will save *The Herald*, that's why!' he bellowed, thrusting a sheet of paper under Annie's nose.

'Look closer!' her dad insisted.

And she did.

Suddenly, before her very eyes, words appeared on the page.

'Well, maybe not exactly . . .' said
the News Editor, from inside a giant
tub of ice cream.

Chapter 7

That night, *The Hogsville Herald* was printed with Ivana's ink. The papers rolled off the presses and were delivered to newsagents all over the town.

The next morning, to the townsfolk's surprise, every page of *The Herald* was bursting with good news!

Whoever
you were,
it told
you just
what you
wanted
to know.

The News Editor, the Gardening Editor and the Sports Editor were delighted. Not only did the paper sell out by coffee time, but each copy had a flattering article all about them!

Before long, people from the neighbouring towns of Pigston, Sowley, Snout and Trotter were clamouring for copies!

The printing presses whirled day and night, and truckloads of Ivana's ink rumbled into town. All over the country, people were reading *The Hogsville Herald!*

One day, a passing French tourist saw a copy . . .

He took it to Paris and showed his friend, who showed his niece in Corfu. She showed her cousin in Mozambique, and he showed his aunt in Peru!

The whole wide world wanted to read *The Herald*. And it wasn't just people . . .

Chapter 8

No one read the other newspapers any more. After all, wouldn't you rather read good news instead of bad news?

Soon, people were too busy reading to talk to each other. No-one went to work any more – not even at *The Hogsville Herald*. Ivana invented computers to run the printing presses and robotic paper boys and mechanical paper girls to deliver *The Herald*.

The problem was, what people wanted to believe was the truth, was very different from the actual truth.

Millions of trees had been chopped down to make enough paper . . .

. . . and smoke from the ink factories polluted everything.

The whole world was in a terrible mess, but no-one even noticed.

One day, some aliens from the
planet Nice landed in Trafalgar
Square, London.

But no-one was listening. Not
Nelson on his column, nor the
pigeons in the square.

Sadly the aliens returned to their
Ps and zoomed off to sail the cosmic
seas.

At last they landed on a sad planet
called Strife, in a galaxy far away.
Now its name is planet Happy, and
its people are contented and gay!

Chapter 9

Meanwhile, Annie, the News Editor's daughter, sat in her room reading *The Herald*. She had just finished an article about how she'd discovered a new colour, and was about to begin another about the six unicorns living in her garage, when she had a thought . . .

Annie put down the paper. For the first time in ages, she saw beyond the end of her nose . . .

She couldn't believe her eyes! She'd been stuck behind the paper for so long, everything around her had changed.

The garden . . .

. . . her pet goldfish, Susan . . .

. . . her hair!

Annie raced around the house, until at last she found him, lying on the kitchen floor like a beached whale.

But the News Editor was too busy munching and moaning to do anything.

Then Annie had an idea.

Chapter 10

First Annie found out where Ivana lived, by looking in her dad's address book under the letter 'I'. Then she ran over to twenty-three Dripping Street and hammered at Ivana's door.

Annie stepped inside.

She found the inventor sitting in
the kitchen.

Ivana was looking rather sad.

Ivana was the only person on the
planet who hadn't been reading
The Hogsville Herald; she'd been
too busy inventing things – like
slippers made from cheese – to
notice what was going on!

Annie told her how the world was falling apart.

'Oh dear,' said Ivana mournfully.

'Snag?' asked Annie.
'What snag?'

Because she was always losing her Lucky Thinking Cap in her laboratory, Ivana had put it upstairs in her hat collection. But her collection was so vast, she couldn't find it anywhere.

Can you spot it in the picture below?

Found it? Good! Now we can carry on with our story.

Ivana got down to work while, outside the laboratory door, Annie anxiously paced up and down.

Two days later, Ivana emerged.

Chapter 11

Ivana held out her hand and
pointed to nothing at all.

'Er . . . what is it?' Annie asked.

'Oh, of course!' said Annie, who was
beginning to think that Ivana was a
very mad little girl.

'But first we must put a drop of it into every barrel of transmogrificational ink in the world,' said Ivana. 'Tonight!'

Ivana attached a strange device to Chester's head.

North, south, east and west they
went, to too many places to mention,
and into each barrel of ink they
dripped a drop of Ivana's invention.

By midnight their job was done.

The next morning, Annie picked up
a copy of the latest *Hogsville Herald*.
It didn't look much different to her,
but when she opened it up . . .

. . . she saw . . .

'Clever, isn't it?' said Ivana, in a know-it-all sort of way.

'What, so instead of reading the newspaper, you see through it?' said Annie.

At that moment, people everywhere were seeing through their morning papers. And they didn't like what they saw.

Fortunately, it wasn't too late.

New trees were planted, and the
smoke-belching ink factories were
closed down. Everyone felt very
cross with themselves for being so
foolish, and promised not to let it
happen again.

Chapter 12

A little while later the News Editor
jogged round to Ivana's house.
Since listening to the truth about
eating well, he was full of health
and vigour.

He invited Ivana over to his house
for a banquet that evening.

'Hmm . . .' said Ivana, 'I'm kind
of busy inventing a hamster-
powered hair drier, but on second
thoughts . . .'

It was a meal fit for a Queen.

After the oozing chocolate cake,
but before the melon stuffed with
blueberry ice cream, the News
Editor filled their glasses with pink
lemonade and proposed a toast.
'To Annie and Ivana!' he said.

'I can't thank you enough for what you've done!' he gushed. 'Please let me give you something!'

'Now let me see . . .' mused Ivana. 'I think I'd like a book written about me!'

'Consider it done!' boomed the News Editor. Then he turned to his daughter.

'Oh, I don't want anything, really!'
she shrugged.

'I'll sleep on it,' Annie said, and the
next morning, when her dad came
down for breakfast, a note was
waiting for him on the kitchen
table . . .

Chapter 13

In your hands, you hold Ivana's wish. But guess what? She couldn't find her Lucky Thinking Cap when she was posing for the cover. Can you?

Now that our story is at an end, it's time for the moral. But because this is the Best Book Ever, you can choose it! Just pick a moral from the selection below, or else go ahead and make up your own!

a It's better to face the truth, than to ignore it.

b Don't believe everything you read.

c Geniuses lose caps.

Oh, and one more thing!

Page 27 wasn't really printed with transmogrificational ink – I was just trying to be clever. No book can be that good, not even the Best Book Ever!